You are about to enter the

Wonderful World of

Alfie Green

On his ninth birthday Alfie
Green got a very special present
– a magical book left
by his grandad.
The book gives Alfie special
powers and opens a whole new
wonderful world ...

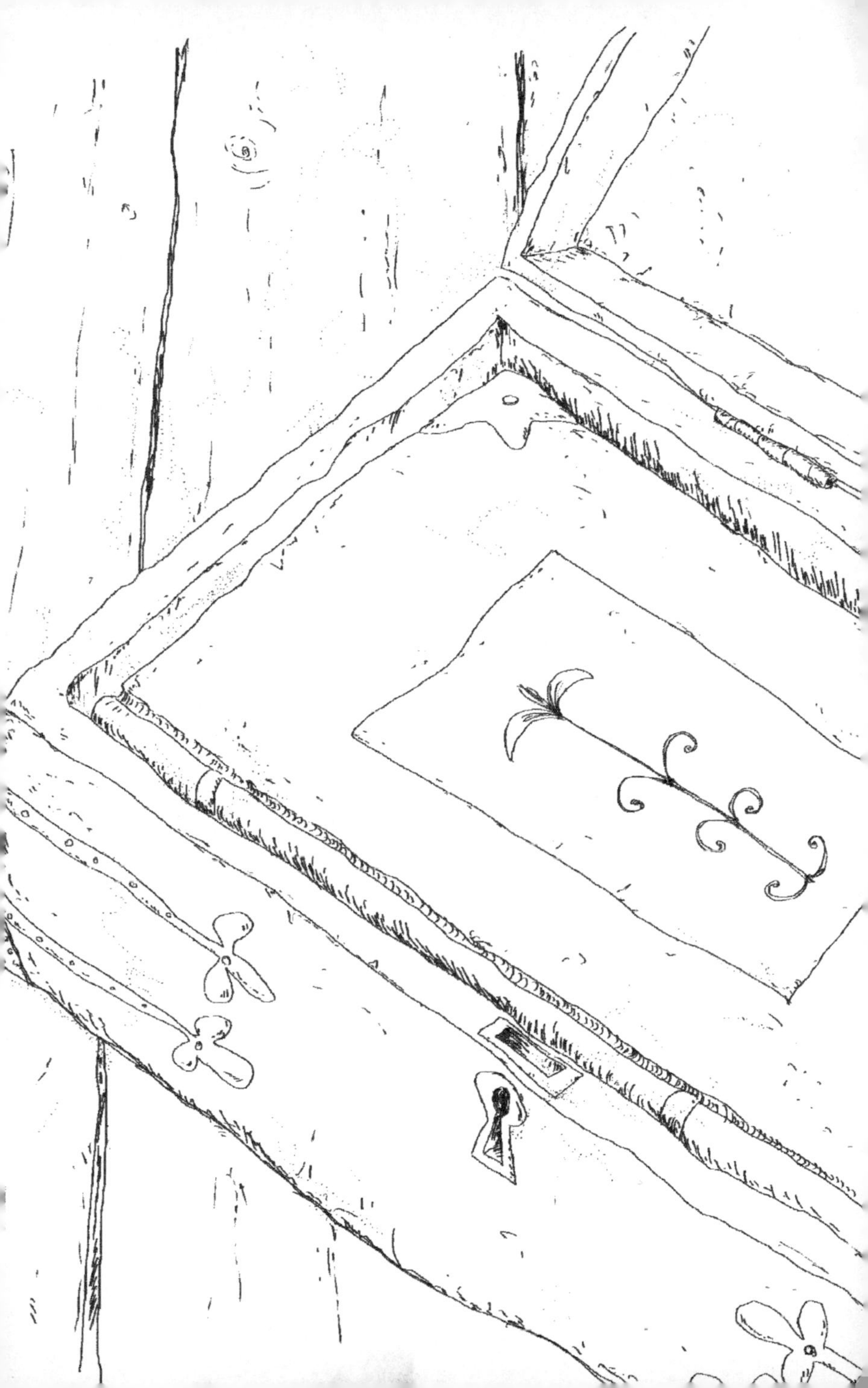

JOE O'BRIEN is an award-winning gardener who lives in Ballyfermot in Dublin. This is his third book about the wonderful world of Alfie Green.

DEDICATION

The *Alfie Green* series is dedicated to my son, Ethan, who in his short time in this world taught me to be strong, happy and thankful for the gift of life. Thank you, Ethan, for the inspiration to write.

Alfie Green and the Bee-Bottle Gang is dedicated to my wife, Mandy, whose encouragement makes all of this possible.

ACKNOWLEDGEMENTS:

A big thank you to all at The O'Brien Press, to Jean Texier, and, of course, to my readers.

* * *

JEAN TEXIER is a storyboard artist and illustrator. Initially trained in animation, he has worked in the film industry for many years.

Alfie Green

and the BEE-BOTTLE GANG

Joe O'Brien

Illustrated by Jean Texier

This paperback edition first published 2007 by The O'Brien Press Ltd.,
12 Terenure Road East, Rathgar, Dublin 6, Ireland.
Tel: +353 1 4923333; Fax: +353 1 4922777
E-mail: books@obrien.ie
Website: www.obrien.ie
First published in 2006 by The O'Brien Press Ltd.
Reprinted 2012.

ISBN: 978-1-84717-054-5

British Library Cataloguing-in-Publication Data
O'Brien, Joe
Alfie Green and the Bee-Bottle Gang
1. Green, Alfie (Fictitious character) - Juvenile fiction
2. Magic - Juvenile fiction 3. Children's stories
I. Title II. Texier, Jean
823.9'2 [J]

3 4 5 6 7 8 9 10
12 13 14 15 16

The O'Brien Press receives
assistance from

Editing, typesetting, layout, design: The O'Brien Press Ltd.
Illustrations: Jean Texier
Printed by Bercker in Germany

CONTENTS

CHAPTER 1

Buzz, Buzz!

The sun shone through the windows of Budsville School, right onto Alfie Green's desk. Alfie was melting like an ice-pop in a glasshouse.

'Add a half of a third of a ...' Alfie's teacher, Mrs Cummiskey, was babbling on about fractions.

Alfie hated maths, and most of all he hated fractions. He wished he was in the park, playing football with his pal, Fitzer.

'Alfie Green! What's the answer?'

Alfie didn't even know what the question was.

'Eh ... um ... three???'

The bell for going-home time rang. Saved! Alfie thought gratefully.

Everybody rushed for the door.

'Not you, Alfie.' Mrs Cummiskey stopped him. 'You will stay back for ten minutes and write: "I must pay attention in class" twenty times on the blackboard.'

Ten whole minutes!!

It seemed to take ten HOURS, but at last Alfie was finished. He wiped his chalky hands on his pants, grabbed his schoolbag and ran.

Alfie was going through Laurel Park when he heard a very loud buzzing noise. It was coming from the hebe bush near the gates. As he got closer he saw hundreds of bees circling around the top of the bush. They sounded very angry.

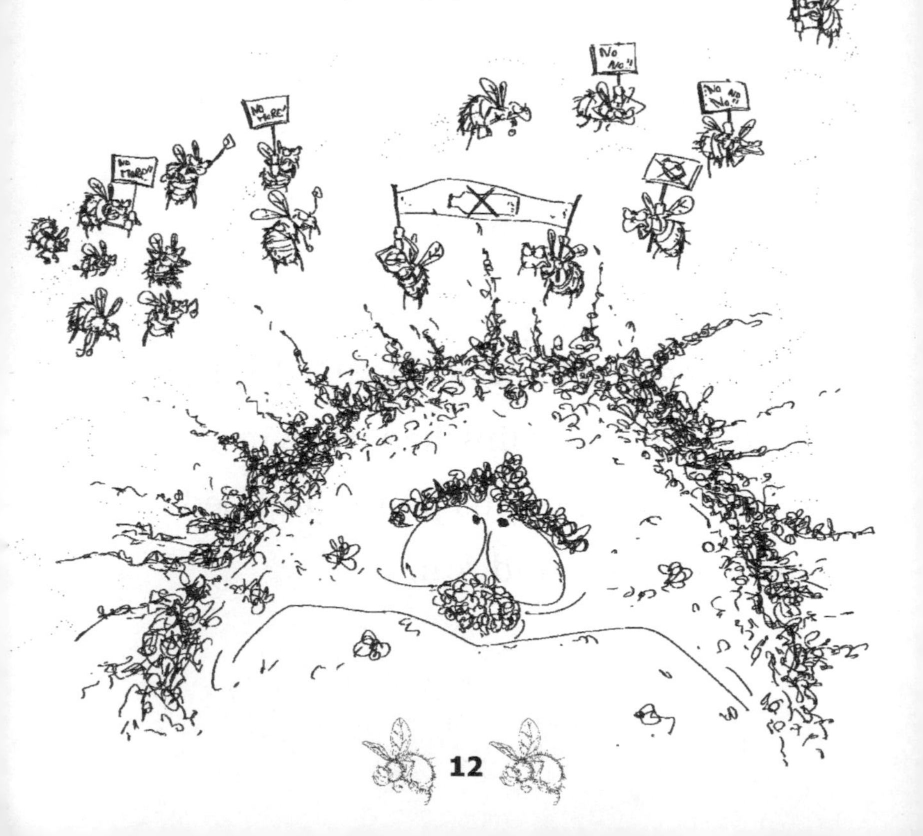

'What's wrong with the bees?' he asked the hebe.

'They're having a meeting,' the bush explained.

'A meeting? About what?'

'They're planning to leave Laurel Park because of the Bee-Bottle Gang,' said the hebe.

He told Alfie that a gang of kids had been in the park every day that week, trapping bees in bottles and jam-jars.

'But what do they do with them?' Alfie asked.

'They don't DO anything with them,' the hebe replied. 'They just leave them in the bottles until they die.'

'That's really cruel!' Alfie was shocked. 'I'll have to find a way to stop them.'

CHAPTER 2

The Bee-Bottle Gang

Alfie threw his schoolbag at the bottom of the stairs and went into the kitchen.

'Pick up that bag, Alfie,' his mother said. 'Your granny will break her neck. And why are you so late? Dilly-dallying in the park again, I suppose?'

'Yes, Mam,' Alfie said. 'Sorry.'

Well, it was *mostly* the reason why he was late, so Alfie didn't mention anything about being kept back to do lines.

'Have I time to go over to Fitzer's?'

'All right, but your dinner will be ready in an hour.'

Fitzer's mother answered the door.

'Is Fit ... I mean, Dean, in?'

'DEANNNN!' Mrs Fitzpatrick shouted.

Alfie's dad said that Mrs Fitpatrick's voice would make a great car alarm. Alfie's ears were riNGing.

'What's the story, Alfie?' Fitzer asked.

'Are you coming to the park for a game?' asked Alfie.

'Nice one!' said Fitzer, and he got his football from under the stairs.

On the way, Alfie told Fitzer about the Bee-Bottle Gang.

'I don't like bees,' Fitzer said. His nose had swollen up like a balloon last summer when he had been stung by a bee.

'I know,' Alfie said. 'But what would happen if everyone went around killing bees? There'd be no more bees. And no more honey!'

‘Oh.’ Fitzer loved honey – honey and banana sandwiches, runny honey on his porridge, drippy honey on chocolate ice-cream …

When they got to the park they saw some kids from their school messing on the slide. Jason Walsh, known as Whacker, was coming down head-first. Adam Burke was hanging on to his ankles and Stephen O'Leary and Emily Farrell followed.

Three glass bottles and a jam-jar lay in the grass by the play area. Alfie could see small shapes flying around inside.

Jason and his pals were the Bee-Bottle Gang!

'Keep a lookout, Fitzer,' Alfie said, dropping to the grass. 'I'm going to save the bees.'

He crawled through the grass and began unscrewing the tops of the bottles. Just as the last bee flew out, there was a shout.

'**Hey!** What do you think you're doing?' Whacker Walsh roared.

'Run, Alfie,' shouted Fitzer, already halfway to the gate.

Alfie was smaller than Whacker, but he was a lot faster.

As he raced out of the park he could hear Whacker yelling:

'I'll get you for this, Green.'

CHAPTER 3

A PLAN

Next morning, Whacker Walsh and his gang were waiting for Alfie and Fitzer outside the school gates.

'You're dead meat, Alfie Green,' said Whacker, and he grabbed hold of Alfie's shirt.

Just then, Principal Boggins arrived on his bike.

'Walsh, get into class NOW, and come to my office after school,' he yelled.

Whacker let Alfie go. 'I'll get you two later.'

'No you won't,' replied Alfie, cheekily. 'You'll be in detention. Now **BUZZ** off.'

'Nice one, Alfie,' said Fitzer.

'Yeah,' Alfie said, 'but Boggins won't always be there to rescue us.'

After school, Alfie went into the garden shed and took the magical book from the box under the floorboards.

The wise old plant rose up from the first page, his crinkly leaves unfolding and sprouting pointy blue hairs.

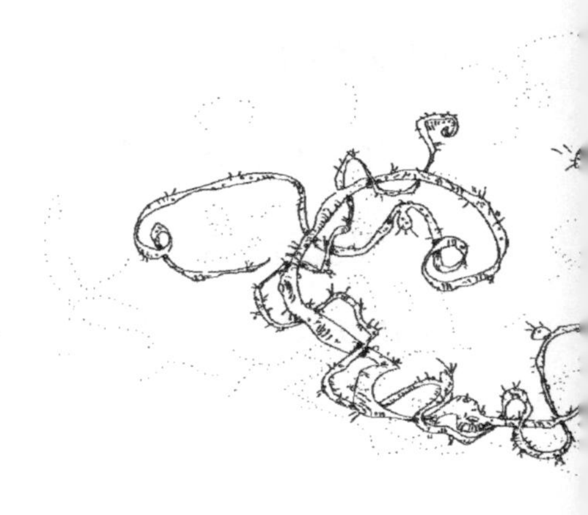

'What can I do for you, Alfie?' asked the plant.

Alfie told him what had happened in the park.

'Well done, Alfie.' The wise old plant was pleased. 'You saved the bees.'

'Only for now,' Alfie said. 'Whacker will be back, and now he's after Fitzer and me, too. What am I going to do?'

'Hmm... just wait a minute.'

The wise old plant began to flick through the pages of the magical book, until he came to a page that said 'Honeycomb Mountain'.

Thousands and thousands of bees were flying in and out of the mountain. It was like a bee city.

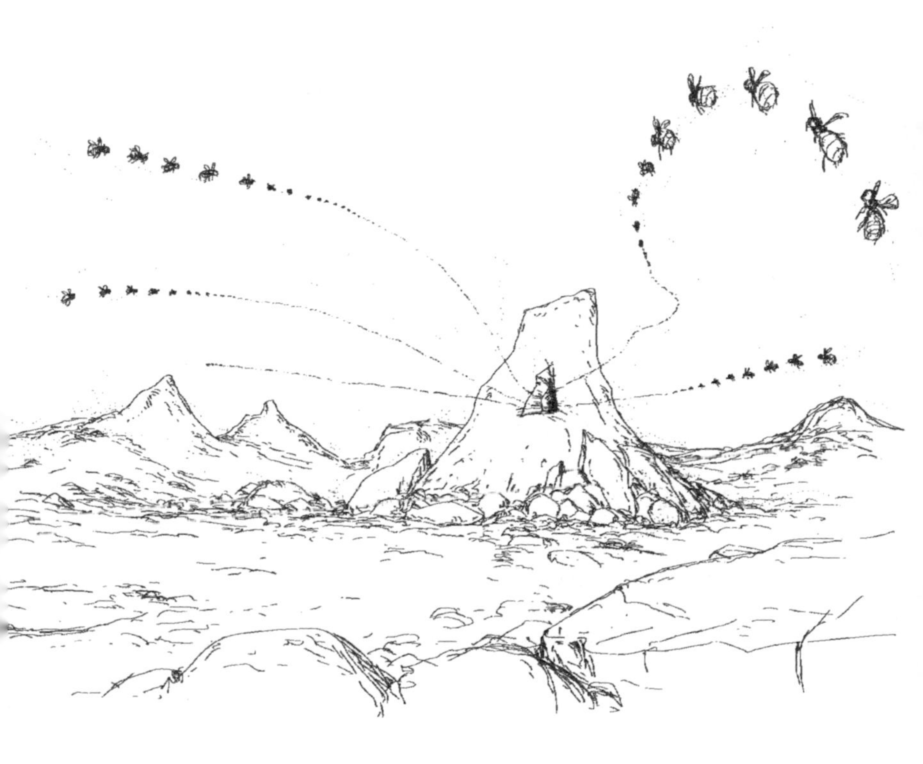

'Wow!' said Alfie. 'That's one buzzy place. I bet the Bee-Bottle Gang wouldn't try to catch bees there.'

'If they did, Alfie, they'd be sorry. Honeycomb Mountain is ruled by the Queen Bee, and she is very well protected. One spray of her warning perfume and her fearsome warrior bees come to her rescue.'

'I've got to get my hands on that perfume!' Alfie said.

'That's exactly what I was thinking,' agreed the wise old plant. 'I'll write a note for the Queen, telling her what you did for the park bees. I'm certain she'll help you. Now, you'll need a bottle.'

Alfie took a bottle off the shelf and held it out.

The wise old plant plucked a hair from one of his leaves and blew it towards Alfie. The hair glided over to Alfie's bottle and turned itself around three times.

With each turn, the bottle cap unscrewed until it lifted off completely and hovered in the air.

Then the hair fell into the bottle

and the cap twisted back on. Alfie watched in amazement as the hair broke into little pieces that became letters, which spun around inside the bottle.

'Off you go, Alfie,' said the wise old plant.

'And don't forget to take your crystal orchid with you to bring you back.'

Then he disappeared into the book, which closed with a

Alfie took his crystal orchid out of the biscuit tin and put it in his pocket. He opened the door of the shed and stepped out into Arcania.

CHAPTER 4

Back to Arcania

'Now, how do I get to Honeycomb Mountain?' Alfie said out loud.

'Can I help?'

A face popped out from behind a tree. It was Paddy the spade O'Toole.

'Paddy! Am I glad to see you! Are Mick and Vinny and Jimmy with you?'

Mick the hoe, Jimmy the clippers and Vinny the fork had helped Alfie on his last adventure in Arcania.

'Mick and Vinny are helping some twisted turnips deal with an invasion of exploding weeds,' Paddy explained. 'And the last time I spotted Jimmy, he was chasing a Snapping Dragon back into Sleepy Meadows.'

'What are you doing back here, Alfie?' he added.

Alfie told Paddy about the Bee-Bottle Gang and how he had to get to Honeycomb Mountain.

'Honeycomb Mountain?' Paddy looked puzzled.

'Don't you know where it is?' Alfie was worried.

'Oh, I know where it is all right,' Paddy said, 'But there is something bothering

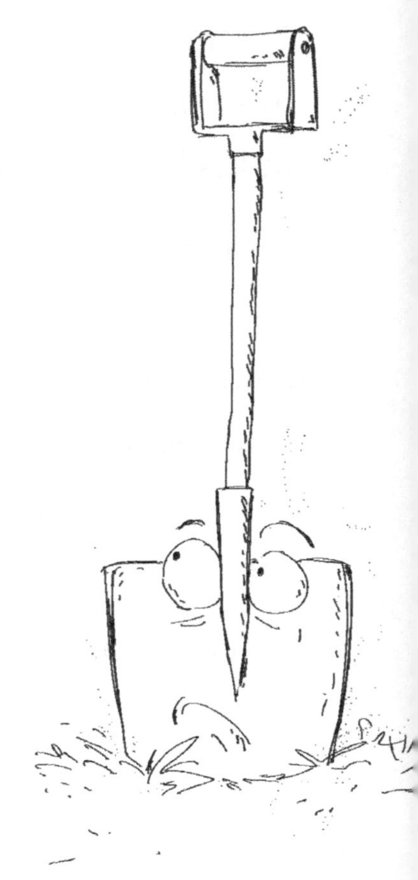

me about Honeycomb Mountain ... I wish I could remember.'

'Why don't we get going?' Alfie suggested. 'It might come to you on the way.'

Paddy and Alfie had been walking for about an hour when they heard a **SPLUT-SPLUT-SPLUTTERING** noise overhead, a bit like an old car breaking down.

'Duck, Alfie!' Paddy shouted suddenly, and they both threw themselves flat on the ground.

CHAPTER 5

Brroom ... Brroom

BANG! Out of the sky and into a tree crashed what looked like a broom plant.

'Wicked! A Flying Broom. How cool is that?' Alfie ran over to help the dazed aviator.

'Are you okay?'

'Fine. I just ran out of fuel,' answered the Broom, picking himself up. He brushed over to a heap of soil, where he dug his roots in deep.

'What are you doing?' asked Alfie.

'I'm re-fuelling,' said the Broom. Soon his branches straightened and his leaves untangled.

BRROOOM
BRROOOM
BRROOOM ...

The Broom blasted out of the soil and flew straight up in the air.

Then he came back down and hovered over Alfie and Paddy.

'Where are you two going?' he asked.

'We're on our way to Honeycomb Mountain,' Alfie told him.

'HONEYCOMB MOUNTAIN! And just how do you plan to go through Firethorn Valley?'

'Uh-oh,' said Paddy.

Whenever Paddy said 'uh-oh' it meant trouble.

'What now, Paddy?' asked Alfie.

'Firethorn Valley – that's what I couldn't remember before.'

'So?'

'Firethorn Valley,' explained the Broom, 'is the only way into Honeycomb Mountain. No one gets through Firethorn Valley alive.'

'He's right, Alfie,' agreed Paddy.

'But I **have** to get to see the Queen Bee!' Alfie was nearly crying.

'Maybe ...' Paddy said thoughtfully, '... maybe you don't have to *go through* Firethorn Valley.'

'But it's the only way into ...' began the Broom, and then stopped. 'Aha! I think I see what you mean.'

'What?' asked Alfie. 'Would somebody *please* let me in on the secret.'

'Well,' Paddy smiled. 'Instead of going THROUGH Firethorn Valley, you could FLY OVER Firethorn Valley...'

'... on a BROOM,' said the Broom triumphantly.

CHAPTER 6

Up Up and Away

'Doesn't Broom Airlines have seatbelts?' Alfie joked.

'Listen,' said the Broom crossly. 'I'm doing you a favour. Now, are you coming or not?'

Alfie hopped onto the Flying Broom.

BROOM ... BROOM ... BROOM ...

'Good luck, Alfie,' shouted Paddy.

'Yeee-haw' screamed Alfie, as he held on tight to the Broom. 'This is magic.'

They flew over parts of Arcania that Alfie had never seen before. There was no sign of Sleepy Meadows or the evil swamp.

Then Alfie saw smoke up ahead.

'Is that Firethorn Valley?' he asked.

'Hang on, Alfie,' warned the Broom. 'I need to be higher when we go over the valley, to be on the safe side.'

The Broom revved and they rose up and up.

'Wow!' gasped Alfie, looking down. 'Look at all the lights. It's like the runway of an airport. Can't we go down for a closer look?'

'No way!' the Broom was horrified. 'They're not lights, they're the glowing flames of the Firethorn bushes. Do you want to be barbecued?'

'Eh, no,' Alfie said quickly. 'I can see perfectly fine from up here.'

The Broom laughed.

'Don't worry, Alfie. We'll soon be out of the valley.'

SPLUTTER ... SPLUTTER

'What's that noise?'

'Noise, what noise?' the Broom said. 'Just a small technical problem. Don't worry, we're nearly there.'

SPLUT ... SPLUT ... SPLUT

Alfie got a sinking feeling in his stomach just like when they went over

Heather Hill too fast in his dad's old car.

THEY WERE GOING DOWN

CHAPTER 7

UNDER FIRE!

'Pull up, Broom!' Alfie shouted.

'Eh, I'm afraid I can't,' said the Broom. 'Fuel problems.'

Down, down, lower and lower they flew until Alfie could see right into the red-hot centre of the firethorn bushes.

One bush, taller than the rest, suddenly shouted an order:

'ATTENTION!'

The firethorn bushes straightened themselves up like soldiers on parade.

'AIM!'

The heads of the bushes rose until they were pointing straight at Alfie and Broom.

'Uh-oh,' said Alfie.

'FIRE!'

A shower of blazing thorns flew up from both sides of the valley.

The Flying Broom ducked and dipped from side to side, trying to dodge the deadly thorns.

'Broom, get us out of here!' screamed Alfie.

'It's no use, Alfie. I haven't got the power.'

'FIRE!'

Another bombardment of blazing thorns whizzed around them.

SPLUTTER ... BROOM... SPLUT... BROOM ... BRROOOM ...

'I knew it,' shouted Broom. 'Dirty fuel.'

The Broom revved hard to burn off the dirty fuel and get his engine working again.

'Quickly, Broom,' shouted Alfie. 'We're going to crash.'

'Oh no we're not!'

The Broom revved harder and Alfie lifted his legs up as high as he could as they brushed along the floor of the valley.

Then, **UP UP UP**

'Hurray!' cheered Alfie.

CHAPTER 8

Honeycomb Mountain

'Look, Broom,' Alfie pointed. 'That must be the entrance to Honeycomb Mountain.'

Up ahead, hundreds of bees were flying in straight lines in and out of a huge tunnel in the rock.

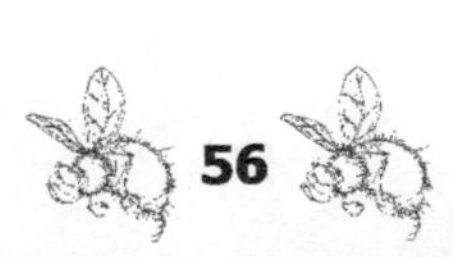

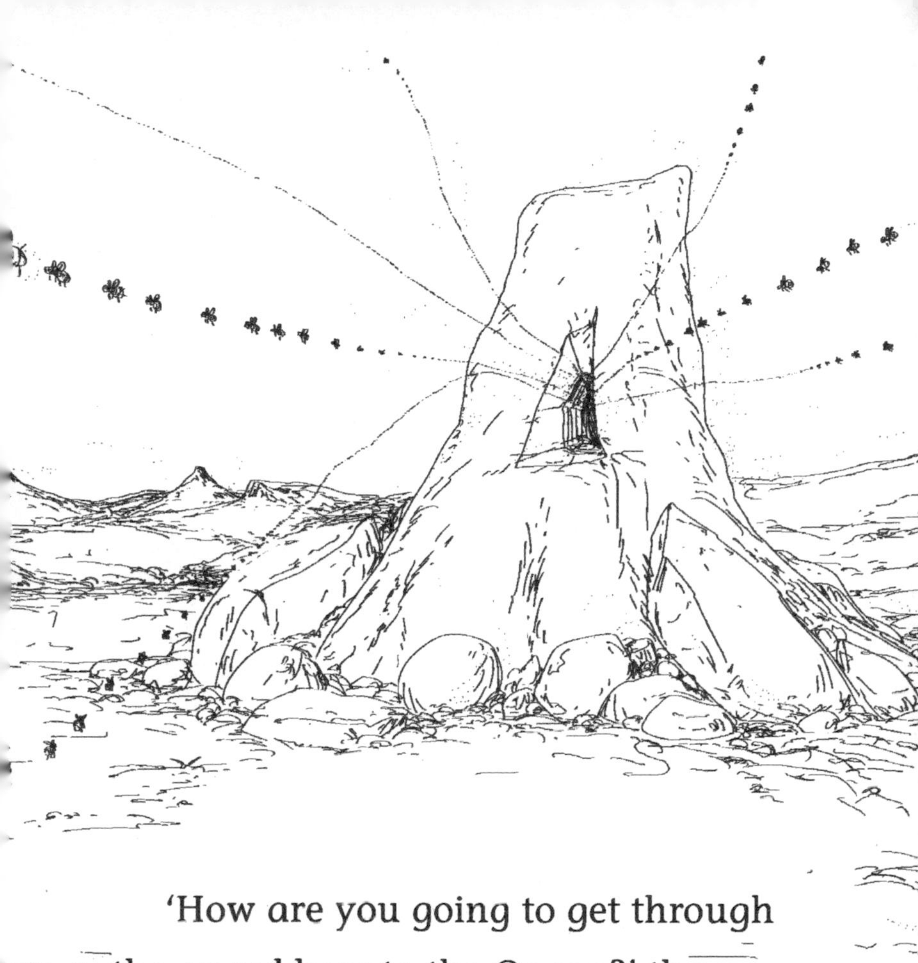

'How are you going to get through the guard bees to the Queen?' the Broom asked.

'I've got a note,' Alfie explained. 'I just hope it works.'

He showed the Broom the bottle with the spinning letters.

'Ah, yes,' the Broom nodded.

'What?' asked Alfie.

'You won't have any trouble with the bees, Alfie. That note is written in Arcanum.'

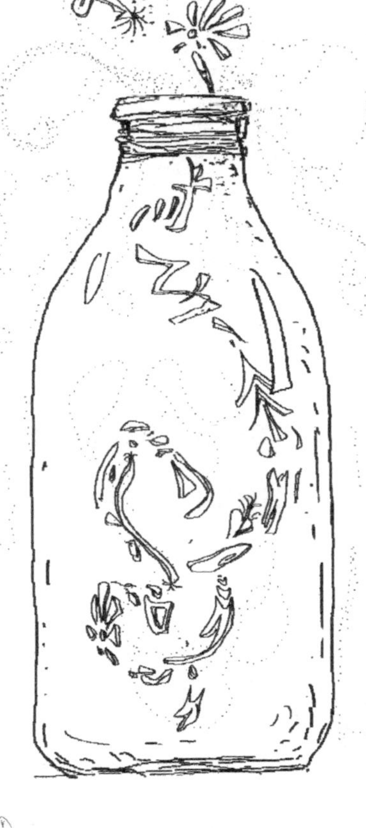

'Arcanum?' Alfie asked. 'Is that the language of Arcania?'

'Sort of. It has a code that all plants and insects understand and respect. Hold it up high, Alfie, so the bees will see.'

The Broom and Alfie joined a line of bees heading into the mountain.

As they approached the entrance, four armed bee guards stopped them.

Crikey! thought Alfie. They're HUGE!

A guard with a vicious-looking stinger approached Alfie and inspected the message in the bottle. He signalled to the other guards, and they flew, one on either side of Alfie and Broom, guiding them through a waxy tunnel that led all the way to the Queen.

If Alfie thought that the guards were big, he was speechless when he saw the Queen Bee.

She was **ENORMOUS**.

Broom set Alfie down gently on the rock floor and gave him a little push.

'Go on,' he said. 'She won't bite you.'

That's just what Alfie was afraid of. Slowly he walked over to the Queen. Looking up anxiously, he unscrewed the cap of the bottle.

The spinning letters whirled upwards and then arranged themselves into the note from the wise old plant.

The Queen read the message. Her huge head bent down towards Alfie and he could hear his knees knocking together in fright. Then she smiled at him and touched the note with her front leg.

The note sparked for a second and then vanished.

A sweet-smelling mist rose up from the spark, drifted over to Alfie and disappeared into his bottle.

Alfie had his perfume.

Alfie nodded a thank-you to the Queen, then said goodbye to Broom.

'Are you sure you don't need a lift, Alfie?'

'No thanks, Broom, I'll be all right now. Thank you for your help.'

Alfie reached into his pocket, took out his crystal orchid, grasped it tightly and closed his eyes.

There was a blinding flash of light. Then he was home.

CHAPTER 9

Whacked

The next morning, Alfie called for Fitzer on his way to school and they took their usual route through the park.

Fitzer was worried. 'What will we do about Whacker?' he asked.

'Don't worry, Fitzer,' said Alfie. 'We'll be grand.'

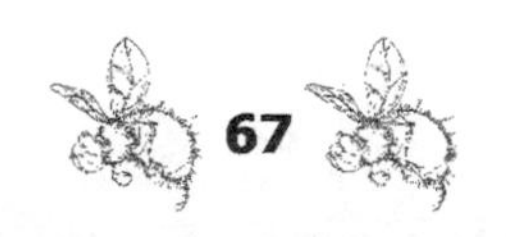

'Grand? Are you mad, Alfie? Whacker is going to go ballistic after what happened yesterday.'

'You got that right, Fitzpatrick,' said a voice.

Whacker and his gang came out from behind the hebe bush.

Alfie laughed.

'What's so funny, Green?' asked Whacker.

'You and your three clowns,' Alfie said.

Fitzer nearly fainted. Alfie's

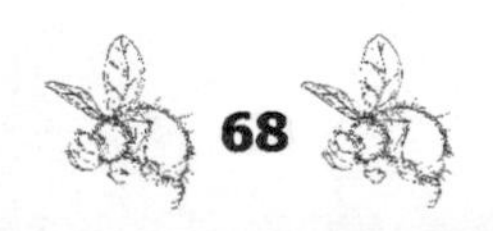

completely lost it, he thought.

Whacker's face went as red as a beetroot.

'WHAT!!!!'

Alfie kept his cool.

'I'm going to make sure your bee-killing days are over, Whacker,' he said, reaching into his bag.

'Oh yeah? You and whose army?' Whacker sneered.

Alfie unscrewed the cap of the bottle.

A dark cloud appeared from nowhere. It formed into a V shape, and then dived.

'Ow!' screamed Emily Farrell.

'My neck! My ear!' yelled Adam Burke.

'Get off!' shouted Stephen O'Leary.

Whacker's gang turned on their heels and ran.

The V shape headed for Whacker Walsh.

'I was only kidding, Alfie,' said a trembling Whacker. 'Call them off!'

He raced down the path, followed by the black cloud of the Queen's warrior bees.

'Ouch! Ooh! Aaagh!'

Alfie screwed the cap back on the bottle and the cloud rose into the air and disappeared.

'How? What?' Fitzer was stunned.

'Come on, Fitzer. We'll be late for school.'

The hebe bush watched the two pals head off and smiled. Thanks to Alfie Green, he'd seen the last of the Bee-Bottle Gang. The park bees were safe again.

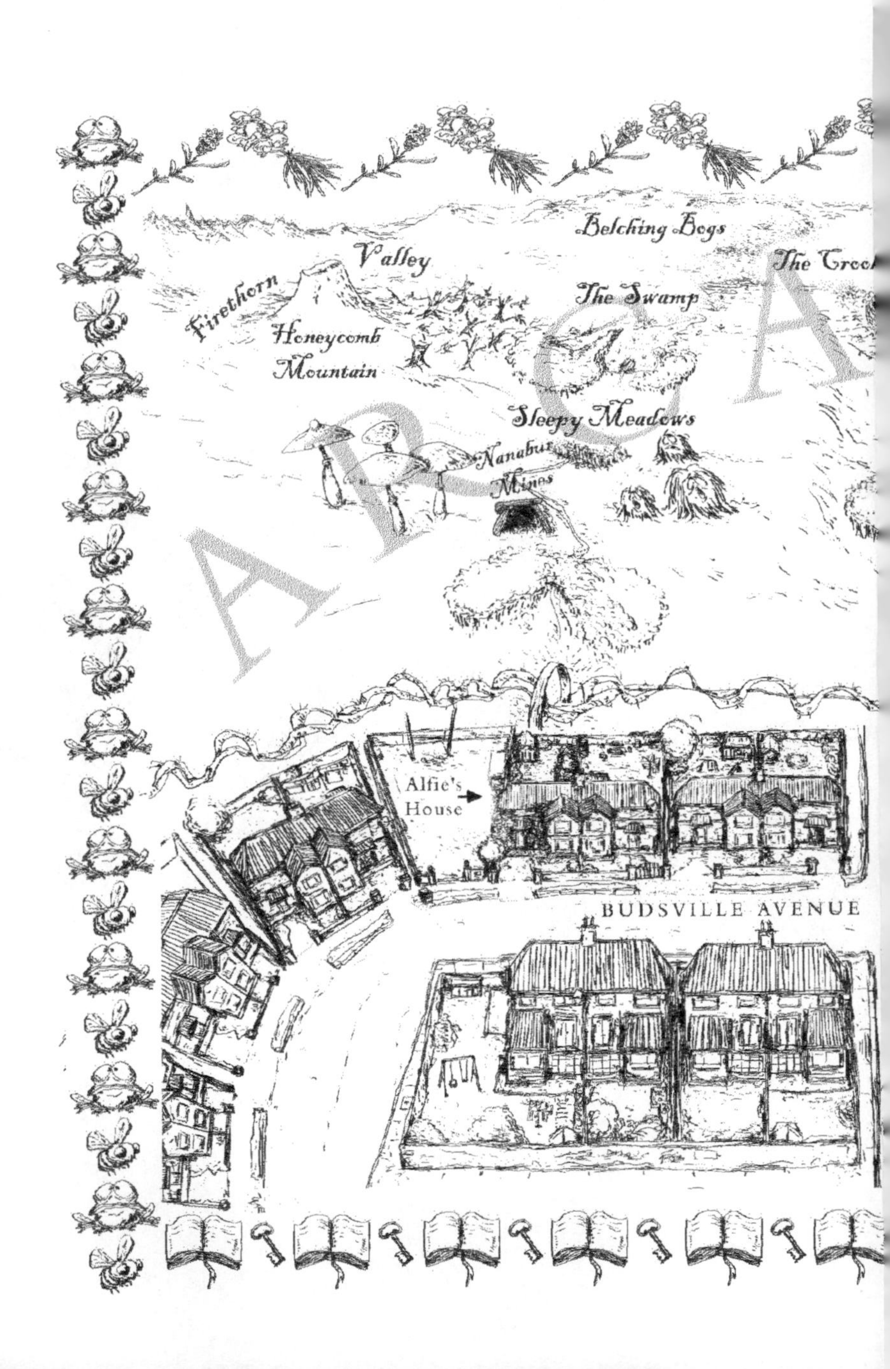

Belching Bogs
Valley
Firethorn
The Swamp
Honeycomb
Mountain
Sleepy Meadows
Nanabur
Mines
Alfie's
House
BUDSVILLE AVENUE

The
Wonderful World of
Alfie Green
SYCAMORE ROAD
LAUREL PARK
BUDSVILLE
PRIMARY
SCHOOL

READ ALFIE'S OTHER GREAT ADVENTURES IN:

Alfie Green and the Magical Gift

A rusty key opens a dusty box hidden in Alfie's grandad's shed. Inside is an old, old book — with magical powers. The book promises Alfie a gift, but first he must take the crystal flower across Sleepy Meadows full of Snapping Dragons to the crooked tree that is guarded by Giant Hogweeds!

Alfie Green and a Sink Full of Frogs

Hundreds of tiny eyes peep up at Alfie Green from the sink in his garden. Frogs! Who invited them? And when the frogs tell their friends and relations about their great new swimming pool, the place is invaded. Alfie needs help — fast. This is a

Alfie Green and the Fly-Trapper

Alfie's house is invaded by flies. His fly-trap plant is too small to eat them all so the wise old plant uses magic to make it bigger. Then it gets BIGGER and BIGGER and BIGGER. Nothing is safe! Alfie decides the only place for the Giant Fly-Trapper is in the Belching Bogs in Arcania.

Alfie Green and the Monkey Puzzler
The circus has come to town. But it's no ordinary circus, it's Monty's Marvellous Monkey Circus and all the performers are monkeys! All the kids from Budsville are really excited, except for Alfie who suspects all is not what it seems ...

Alfie Green and the Conker King
Alfie would love to win the School Conker Championship. But with Conor Hoolihan on his team and Whacker Walsh cheating all the time, he has no chance. He needs to find a Super Cracking Conker, and he needs to find one fast.

Alfie Green and the Supersonic Subway
When the Emerald Cactus in the Desert of Doom explodes, Budsville is covered in sparkling green sand ... Soon the evil Desert Elves will arrive on their Scorpion Chariots. How can Alfie stop them?

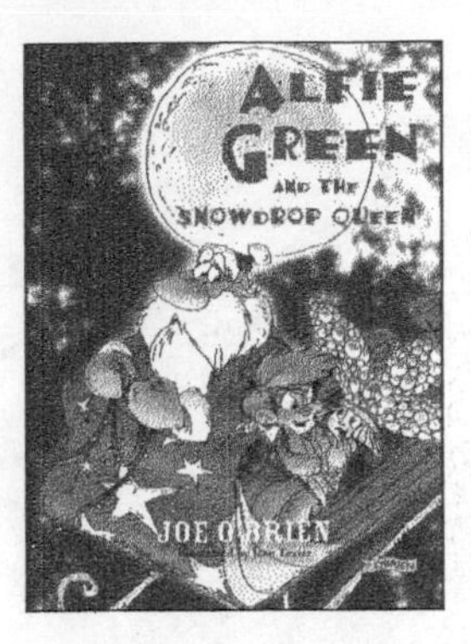

Alfie Green and the Snowdrop Queen

It's Christmas Eve in Budsville and Alfie Green wishes it would snow. There is one person who can help his wish come true – the Snowdrop Queen. But she lives near the top of the Perilous Peaks in Arcania. This is a place too dangerous for his friends, the tools, who often help him on his adventures in Arcania. So how can Alfie get there? Maybe Santa will help...

Alfie Green and the Chocolate Cosmos

Budsville's chocolate fair cancelled? No way, Alfie decides. The wise old plant tells him of the Roaring Rainforest in Arcania where he can collect chocolate seeds. But it won't be easy. Alfie has to brave the vicious Spider Plants, the Forest Ogre and the Chocolate Vine waiting to catapult him through the gateway of the Chocolate Cosmos. Not even his crystal orchid will be able to save him then.